IN THE MARSHAL'S ARMS

CHAPTER 1

U.S. Marshal Rhys Burgess sat on his horse and looked down on the sad little ranch house below. It didn't look like much, certainly not like the home of one of the most ambitious bank robbers of the past decade.

The man he'd watched die last month.

The yard was barren, with a shriveled garden and unpainted house, barn, outhouse and chicken coop. No one was around, no hands, which made Rhys's plan easier, but made him wonder about the woman who worked this land on her own.

But the bank robber Edward Colby hadn't worked alone, and his brother was still at large. Rhys had heard Luke would come here, to the mistress he and his brother shared, to keep a low profile, and possibly bring some of the profits from their last job. And when he did, Rhys would be here waiting. He just had to convince

Maddy Colby, the mistress who had taken the brothers' name.

He nudged his horse forward, down the hill.

A dog started barking frantically. Rhys scanned the yard, but saw nothing until the dog exploded from the house, stopping at the edge of the weathered porch and standing stiff-legged. The woman herself followed, a rifle in one hand, and shaded her eyes as she watched him approach.

Because she stood in the shadows, he didn't get a good look at her until he pulled Bathsheba up in the yard. When he did, she was nothing like he expected. Her dress was a plain worn calico day dress, and she was younger than he thought, not as tough as he would have thought the mistress of two outlaws would be. It looked like—did she have freckles?

"Help you?" she asked, lifting her hand to the auburn knot at the back of her head.

"I'm looking for work." He inclined his head toward the house. "Looks like you need some help around here."

She curved her shoulders forward in a defensive posture. "I don't have money to pay for help."

No money. It looked like she was telling the truth, but maybe it was just a plea for privacy. "Doesn't matter. I'll work for room and board. I been on the road a long time, ma'am, and I just need a place to stop for a bit."

She shifted the rifle into both hands. "You in trouble?"

He wondered if she knew how to use the gun. He

was fairly certain Edward Colby would make sure of that. "No, ma'am."

She glanced behind her, but the intelligence he'd gathered in town already told him no one else was here. She was right to be wary, a woman alone out here.

"I'm not looking for help."

"What about protection?" He nodded at the mongrel. "I doubt he's a lot of good to you."

"I haven't had any trouble so far. All I need is for him to give me the alarm. I'm a fair shot." She lifted the rifle higher, as if planning to give him a demonstration.

"I believe that you are." He eased Bathsheba back just a bit, in case he had to bolt.

"My husband will be home soon."

He knew that wasn't true, but he decided to play along. Cautiously, he swung out of the saddle, facing her.

"He left you a lot of work here on your own. I could help you get it looking nice for when he returns. He'd appreciate that, don't you think?"

She lowered the rifle a bit, probably because it was growing heavy, and her eyelashes flicked. "How do I know you're a good guy?"

He wanted to tell her she should be able to tell a good guy from a bad guy after being involved with Edward and Luke Colby. Instead he said, "You don't. And I don't blame you for not taking my word for it. If it makes you feel better, I'll do some work for a meal and be on my way."

Her lips turned down and she lowered the rifle to her side. "You could do that. But I'll be watching you."

Relief ran through him and he patted his horse's neck. One day was a beginning. "You mind if I tend to Bathsheba first?"

"Go ahead." She gestured in the direction of the barn.

As he led his horse away, he wondered if she didn't get lonely out here, with only a dog for company. Honestly, he'd expected more of a fight.

A team of horses were the only occupants of the barn, which was in a sad state of disrepair. He unsaddled Bathsheba, rubbed her down, then gave her some grain, fed the team as well, and headed toward the house.

At the edge of the porch stood a curtained-off contraption with pipes and wooden posts, surrounded on three sides by muslin curtains. He peered inside to see the ground was moist. Above him hung something that looked like a giant watering can. He stepped back to see that the watering can was attached to a cistern.

"It's a shower," Maddy Colby said from the porch.

Rhys used every bit of training not to jump in surprise.

"When you need to cool off, or if you don't want to haul water for a bath, you bathe here." She approached warily, reached past him and tugged a rope. Water streamed out of the giant watering can in an even flow and splashed on the earth below.

"Your husband make that for you?"

"No, I did it," she said with some pride. "I have running water in my house, too."

He wasn't sure whether or not that was an invitation. "Sounds like a fine thing."

She nodded and he took a look at her in the sunlight. Her auburn hair was a myriad of colors—so many he wondered if two strands were the same. Her big brown eyes were long-lashed and her nose had a cute little slope, with a dusting of freckles. Pretty pink lips just begged for a man's kiss. Her dress was a faded calico, but it hugged her full breasts and nipped in at her narrow waist. He was surprised to see she was barefoot beneath her skirts.

How had an idiot like Colby won such a beauty?

"What would you like me to work on first?"

"I've been thinking on that," she said. "I've been trying to repair the roof, but it's a trick to climb around up there in a skirt."

He stepped back to look up at the angled roof. "I can see that. Where are the supplies?"

"Up there already, shingles, hammer and nails. The ladder's around back."

Indeed it was, already leaning against the edge of the house. And when he climbed up the steeply pitched roof to see she'd done a great deal of the work herself, he was impressed.

A few hours—and quite a few swear words later and a throbbing thumb later—Maddy Colby stepped out into the yard and shaded her eyes to look up at him.

"Mr. Burgess. Dinner will be ready in just a bit. Will you come down and take a shower?"

He set the hammer down and sat back on his heels. "I beg your pardon?"

"I—I don't want—just, before you come into the house."

"Ah." He did smell pretty bad, with trail dirt and sweat from being up here in the sun. Texas heat, even in November, could be a bitch. He'd thought about a bath, but he wondered about operating the shower. "Now?"

"Please."

He looked at the work he'd accomplished. Quite a lot but not done. He straightened, his back cricking, his shoulders aching. He hadn't done manual labor like this since he was a kid. He readjusted his hat and headed toward the ladder. When he looked down, she had gone inside.

MADDY STIRRED the gravy with a shaking hand. She hadn't had anyone to cook for in months and she enjoyed the process. She hoped Mr. Burgess had an appetite. In her experience, men did. She hadn't had any interaction with anyone in weeks, and hoped she remembered how without making too much of a fool of herself. She glanced out the front window and her spoon froze.

Mr. Burgess stood at the edge of the porch, close to the shower, and stripped off his undershirt, revealing a muscled chest and shoulders, a vee of black hair covering his chest, tapering down his flat stomach and into his pants. Her mouth went dry at the sight.

Edward Colby, her lover, had been a handsome man, fit, but barrel-chested and hirsute, and his brother Luke, who sometimes shared her bed, was broad-shouldered and heavily muscled. This man was lean, square-shouldered, the muscles in his arms and stomach flexing as he moved. He unbuckled his pants and her womanhood throbbed. It had been too long since she'd had sex. Edward had been killed and Luke hadn't returned for months. The brothers had taken her from the theater, where she'd had regular lovers between her nights on stage. The past few months were the longest she'd gone without a man, and Mr. Burgess was a fine specimen.

What would he think if she walked outside now? If she ran her hand down over his stomach and into his pants, curled her fingers around his cock?

Ridiculous woman. She knew nothing about this man. She should have just had him move on, but she'd invited him on instinct. She did need help around the place. She needed to focus on that.

But those good intentions went to hell when he stripped off his britches. His cock lay heavy against the length of his thigh, and she could almost feel the weight of it in her mouth, the texture of it along her tongue. Sucking cock was one of her specialties. She enjoyed the act, the power it gave her. In her mind's eye, she could see Mr. Burgess's head fall back in pleasure when she knelt before him.

Mr. Burgess turned toward the shower, presenting her with his delicious backside, and fiddled with the rope. He tugged cautiously, then jumped back comically when the water splashed him. He edged toward the water, pulling the rope as he did so. Once he was fully in the shower, he released the rope and picked up the soap she'd left for him. She watched as he lathered his chest, then ran soapy fingers over his scalp, scrubbed his shoulders and thighs and groin. She wished he would allow her to scrub his back, just to feel his hard warm body. Her fingers curled against the window frame as he pulled the rope again and water sluiced over his body, slicking his hair back from his face, revealing strong bones there.

He stepped back onto the porch, picked up the drying sheet she'd left for him, and lifted his head.

She backed away from the window, hoping he hadn't seen her staring.

* * *

RHYS RAPPED at the door of the cabin, feeling like a new man. A great contraption, that shower, better than sitting in a hip bath in his own filth. And after a day on the roof, he felt cool.

Mrs. Colby opened the door, a soft blush coloring her cheeks. She'd changed her dress, he thought. This one seemed to be darker, brought out her eyes. He looked past her to see two plates set on the table. The room itself was tiny, dominated by her bed. In addition to the two chairs at the table, another chair sat close to the stone fireplace on the opposite end from the kitchen, which was around the corner of the L-shaped house, and was just as small.

"It's been a while since I cooked for someone other than myself," she murmured, opening the door wider. "I hope you're hungry."

"Famished." He stepped inside but felt uneasy about closing the door behind him. He was good at listening to his own instincts, and while he didn't think she was a danger to him physically, he was aware that an odd kind of energy heated the air.

"I'm a good cook, and I grow most everything myself." She removed the top from a large pot and steam rose, scented with pork. "I do need to go into town for some supplies. It's been a while, but I think you'll enjoy it."

She served up green beans with chunks of pork, a chunk of meat that fell apart, it was so tender, and sliced up the lightest, airiest bread he'd ever seen. He slathered his piece with a hunk of butter as she watched, pride making her face glow.

"I'd thought your husband would have married you for your beauty," he said when he came up for air. "Now I see he married you for your cooking."

She gave a delighted laugh.

He motioned toward her still-empty plate. "You're not eating?"

"I wanted to make sure you had enough first. I was sure you'd have a large appetite."

Shamed at the way he'd plowed through the dinner, he set down his utensils. "I'm only making a glutton of myself, Mrs. Colby. My apologies for my bad manners."

"Not necessary. There is no greater compliment to a cook than to see a man dig in."

Though the taste of the food lingered and his mouth begged for more, he left his utensils on his plate and watched as she served herself tiny portions that wouldn't keep a bird alive. Frustrated, he took the spoon from her and doubled her portions. She laughed and began to eat.

"How long have you lived here?" he asked, cradling the cup of coffee between his hands as he sat back.

"Almost four years," she said.

"And before that? Where did you live?"

"I was born in the New Mexico Territory, and I worked there for a while before I joined a troop of actors and we moved from place to place before I met Edward."

He knew that, of course. "I imagine this life is quite different."

"It is quiet," she said with a wistful sigh. "But I enjoy having no one to answer to but myself."

"And your husband. Where has he gone?"

She shifted slightly in her chair and focused on her plate. "To Kansas to help his brother."

Kansas, where Rhys and several other marshals had learned about the bank robbery ahead of time, surrounded the bandits, and shot Edward Colby dead in the street. How much did Maddy know about his death? As much as he loathed the man and all he'd done, he didn't want Maddy to know the gruesome details.

"You said he'd be back soon?"

She concentrated on buttering a slice of bread. "He's been gone a while."

For just a moment, he doubted that she knew of Edward's death, but no, he'd spoken to the marshal who'd delivered the news. Had she cried? Did she mourn him?

She looked up then. "What about you? Are you married?"

The question shouldn't have caught him off-guard, but it did. "My wife died a few years back." And he hadn't been able to bring himself to go home since. The life of a marshal had suited him as he grieved.

"No children?"

He shook his head. For that, at least, he could be grateful.

"No, we didn't, either. It's probably a blessing." Regret laced her voice.

He had to change the subject, and struggled for a topic to make her smile. "I should be able to finish the roof tomorrow," he said. "What do you have for me to do next?" Everywhere he looked, the place needed work, but he didn't know what her priorities were.

"The barn likely needs repair as well. I do need a trip into town, but I'm not sure about the state of the wagon."

"I'll take a look after dinner."

She pushed back from the table abruptly. "I made a pie."

That surprised a laugh from him. "You've been busy while I was on that roof."

"It's nice to have someone around to cook for. I usually just make bread for myself. I'm happy to remember I can cook."

Half an hour later, Rhys rose from the table, unable to remember the last time he'd eaten so much. His mother had been a good cook, but he'd left home seventeen years ago, and he'd had to share those meals with three brothers. His wife had been an adequate cook, but Mrs. Colby was clearly talented.

"I'm afraid I didn't leave much for you to put away for tomorrow," he said as she cleared the table.

"That's fine. If we can make it to town, I have no doubt I can make something to please you tomorrow."

"I'll go check on that wagon, then," he said. Best for him to leave this scene before it made him feel too domestic. He couldn't allow that.

CHAPTER 2

A clap of thunder jolted Maddy awake and a moment later, rain drummed on the roof as the sky opened above her. She scrambled for the pots she usually put under the leaky spots, but when she reached each place, no water came through. Mr. Burgess had patched all the worst spots, God bless him.

Lightning flashed and she looked out the window. And the poor man was sleeping in the barn, which had fewer repairs than the house. The roof likely leaked like a sieve. She couldn't allow that. She'd never be able to sleep knowing he was uncomfortable. She shoved her feet in her shoes, wrapped her shawl over her head and around her shoulders, lit a lantern, and hurried out into the storm.

Though it had been raining only a short time, the path between the house and barn was slush. Her lantern was extinguished almost immediately, leaving her dependent on the lightning to guide her way. The mud slowed her progress, which meant the rain drenched her shawl and her hair and her dress by the time she reached the door of the barn. She didn't know what she expected to see, but Mr. Burgess at the stall door, holding a lantern and calming his horse wasn't it.

"Mr. Burgess!" she said, breathless, and he whirled toward her, his hand on his hip, as if he was going for his gun. Had he been wearing it, would he have shot her? Fear iced her nerves. So he was a gunslinger. She should have known he was in trouble. And she'd come down here to welcome him into her house.

His shoulders relaxed when he realized what he'd done. "What are you doing out here in this?"

"I'd worried the roof was leaking and you'd be wet," she said, her gaze drifting to the bed he'd made in the hay which was, indeed, wet. "I came to suggest you bed down in the house."

"Your husband would likely not like that plan."

"My husband would understand," she lied, because she didn't understand her compulsion herself. Mr. Burgess was a man of the outdoors. He'd probably slept outside during worse storms than this. And she knew nothing of him, other than he fixed her roof, ate her food, and was as jumpy as a gunfighter. But he had been polite, had given her no indication that he would hurt her. Was she too trusting?

"It's hardly proper."

She thrust her chin out. "I'm not inviting you to my bed, Mr. Burgess. I'm inviting you into my dry home. You can make your bed on the floor."

"I've slept in worse."

"But tonight you don't have to. It's the least I can offer since you ensured I won't be sleeping in a leaking house."

"I thank you, ma'am."

For a moment, she thought he'd refuse, but then he bent to get his saddlebags.

"I have an oilcloth in here. You should put it on before you go back up to the house."

"I can hardly get any wetter," she said. "You use it and come on now."

Again, he hesitated, then draped the oilcloth over his head, took up the lantern in one hand, her arm in the other, and guided her to the house. The rain lashed sideways, stinging her face and she bent her head toward him to block it. He released her arm and curved his arm around her shoulders, shielding her, urging her forward.

Finally they were on the front porch and he stripped off the oilcloth to hang it on a nearby hook. He stared at her as she did the same with her shawl, then bent to remove her muddy shoes.

"You are a hell of a woman," he said when she unrolled her stockings and draped them over a bench by the door.

She straightened to look at him curiously, and something flared in his eyes. Only then did she realize she wore nothing but her nightgown, made of the thinnest lawn, and she was soaked to the skin. She might as well be naked in front of him. Twin sensations of fear and arousal shot through her. How would he react?

How did she want him to react?

He turned away and opened the door, his jaw tight. Well, then. Of course, he did believe she was married.

She preceded Mr. Burgess into the house, spine straight. "I have some dry bedding you can use, if you'll give me a moment." She headed for the area she'd curtained off for privacy. She shivered out of the wet gown and draped it over the top of the curtain and listened for movement on the other side. He hadn't moved once he'd come in the door, and stood waiting.

"Could you start a fire? There's wood in the fire-place," she asked as she tugged on her day dress with chilled fingers and buttoned the bodice. She didn't usually light a fire when she was asleep, was too afraid of letting it burn, but he seemed alert enough for both of them.

She heard him move about, followed by the crackling of the fire, and emerged from the curtain. She opened the chest at the end of the bed and withdrew some blankets with cold stiff fingers. The floor would be hard beneath them, but he would be dry. She passed the blankets to him and stood in front of the fire, her arms wrapped about herself.

"Do you have another shawl?" he asked, stepping up behind her.

"No, but I'll be fine when I get back into bed. I didn't know the weather was about to change. You came in just the knick of time, didn't you?" She smiled over her shoulder.

"I suppose that's true. You might have been better off sleeping in the barn tonight, as bad off as your roof was." He offered a smile of his own.

She scrambled for something to say. She had been around handsome men before, but something about Mr. Burgess's smile hit her below the heart, making her feel giddy.

"I was thinking more that you'd be stuck out in it somewhere."

"But I'm not," he said, smile fading. "I appreciate your hospitality, but I would feel better if you'd get in bed and warm up. I can take care of the fire, and making my own bed."

She felt awkward crossing the room to her bed, drawing back the covers and sliding inside. She never slept in a dress, but she didn't have another nightdress, and her shift was even more sheer than the nightdress had been. When she'd been in the acting troop, she'd been accustomed to sharing a room with several people, men and women alike. And she'd been with Edward for four years, though he wasn't often home. She hadn't slept with someone else in the room in a long time. She rolled onto her side, facing the wall, but couldn't help listening to him settle down. Did he sleep fully dressed, too? Was he as uncomfortable as she was? When was the last time he'd slept in the same room with a woman? She couldn't imagine he was the celibate type, but neither did she think he was the type to take a mistress.

Goodness, she would never get to sleep speculating about his sexual habits, especially when she couldn't know, since she'd only known him a matter of hours. She tried focusing on the rain on her new roof, the fire in the fireplace and the warmth of the blankets surrounding her, and not on the sound of him settling onto the floor, the evenness of his breathing.

Finally when his soft snores filled the room, she let herself drift to the rhythm, and fell asleep.

WHEN SHE WOKE, sunlight streamed through the windows, and Mr. Burgess was gone. The blankets were folded neatly and placed on top of the chest at the foot of the bed. She hadn't even heard him get up. Now, though, she heard the pounding of a hammer.

She tossed back the heavy covers and swung her legs over the edge of the bed. Despite the fire burning fairly well in the fireplace, a chill bit at her skin even through her dress. She hurried to the stove to light it, hoping to add to the warmth as she made breakfast for Mr. Burgess. She looked out the window and saw the top of his head over the roof of the barn. Past him, she saw the sun higher than she expected—how long had she slept?

She made her ablutions, then cooked up some pork and eggs, frying up bread as she did so. She put the food on a plate, then went to call Mr. Burgess. Her shawl was still wet, so she wrapped a blanket around her and headed to the barn.

He looked down at her from the peak of the roof. He wore two shirts today, but that was his only concession to the colder weather. "Did I wake you?"

She shook her head. "You should have. I would have made you a good breakfast. It's waiting for you now."

He nodded and made his way to the ladder. "We won't be able to make it to town today. The roads are too muddy. No sense putting the horse through that if we can wait another day."

"We can wait," she said as he dropped to the ground beside her.

"You didn't have to make me breakfast. I could have waited until dinner."

She glanced at the sun. "I'm thinking it's close to that time anyway."

He grinned. "Maybe."

"I'm not usually such a lay-about."

"You don't have to explain anything to me. Out here on your own, you can keep your own schedule. I know I do, when I'm on the trail."

"I haven't had anyone else to think about for a while."

"What about your husband?"

Oh, dear. She'd let that slip, hadn't she? That she'd lied because she'd been afraid? If he knew the truth, would he think her vulnerable?

"He hasn't been home in quite a long time."

"Which is why you're expecting him."

"Yes." For some reason, the lie made her stomach sink. She was drawn to him, and if he thought she was married, he'd never allow himself to think of her sexually. But she didn't know him well, and couldn't measure his response to the truth.

RHYS SAT across from the beauty, the image of her in her soaked nightshift burned into his brain, those lush breasts, trim waist, hips perfect for a man's hands. He'd walked into the cabin last night with his cock hard and pleading for a chance to plunge between those curvy thighs. Thank God she'd changed quickly and he'd been able to distract himself by lighting the fire. A trip to town would have been ideal today, but no, he was in the house with her, forcing himself to keep his gaze from her breasts.

The domestic scene didn't help. What kind of woman was she to invite a hired man to her table? Generous, he wanted to think, but she had been a bank robber's lover. He didn't know how much she knew about the Colbys' activities—and it certainly didn't seem that the men had spent the money on her—but he couldn't be too cautious.

"What are you going to be working on today?" he asked as he spooned fluffy eggs into his mouth.

"Laundry will be the big job. Can I wash anything for you?"

"It's a bit cold to be doing laundry."

"Oh, no, I do it in here." She gestured to the deep sink behind her. "I have a way to hook my wringer onto the sink so it will drain to the outside, and when it's too cold, I hang the clothes in the house. The fire dries them quickly enough, though I don't care for the smell. Today is brisk, but I'll probably still hang them outside."

He rose to look at the sink, with its big pump handle. He saw the slot where her wringer would fit on the side of the sink. "Did you rig that as well?"

She shrugged, and her cheeks turned that pretty pink. "I hate hauling water, so, yes."

He traced his finger around the drain hole. "And this leads outside?"

"Yes, it collects in a bucket on the other side of the wall. I can use that for the garden, if need be."

He turned to look at her. "Clever."

"If I could figure out how to hook up a shower in here and heat it, I would. Not much space for that, though." When he just stared, she shrugged again. "I don't sit still very well."

He chuckled. "I can see that." Aware that he was becoming too friendly, he stepped toward the door. "I'd best get back to the roof."

But even as he hammered the rest of the day, he kept an eye on her as she hung out load after load of laundry. Seeing his shirts fluttering in the breeze beside her petticoats was kind of nice. Never had he thought a sight like that would arouse him.

. . .

"The roof on the barn is fixed. I'll sleep out there tonight," Mr. Burgess announced over dinner.

She shook her head. "The wind has died down, which means tonight will be even colder. Stay in here by the fire."

He met her gaze over the lantern. "Your husband would not like it if he came in to find me sleeping a few feet from your bed."

She swallowed. "I doubt he would travel in this weather."

"He might, if he was missing you."

Even if he was alive, that would never happen. Edward always seemed happy to see her, but he had never hurried home to her.

"I don't want to be shot for being in the wrong place at the wrong time."

"He won't be home tonight. I'm sure of it."

Still, Mr. Burgess seemed anxious to leave. Should she tell him the truth?

"I'll feel safer with you in the house," she said.

He considered a moment, then nodded. "We should be able to make it to town tomorrow. After that, do you have any other jobs for me?"

"Are you planning to move on?" Her stomach knotted at the thought of him leaving. She hadn't realized how lonely she was until she had someone else around. She supposed she'd get used to being alone again, but the idea held no appeal.

"Not as long as there's work that needs to be done. I just wanted to know what was next."

"Perhaps I should make you a list." Then horror struck her. Could he read? Her gaze flew to his face to read his expression.

He merely nodded. "That would be fine, as long as it isn't too long."

She laughed, as much in relief as anything. "Did you go to school, or learn to read at home?"

"I learned to read at home because my mother had been a teacher, but I also went to school. I have a particular aptitude for figures."

"Arithmetic was my favorite subject. Geography was my least, until I started traveling from one place to another. I wanted to see where I was in relation to home, so I taught myself."

"Do you have any books in the house?"

"Nothing with stories. I do enjoy a penny dreadful every now and again, but it's been a while."

"I usually have one or two in my pack, but I traded them for some jerky a while back."

"The jerky likely lasted longer," she said with a laugh.

He grinned. "I'll check on the animals and then I'll be back in."

Maddy was nervous as she cleared the table. The hour was early, too early for bed, and she didn't know how to pass the time with another person in the house.

She had no room for entertaining, only her bed and the table.

When Mr. Burgess returned, he checked the wood supply beside the stove, then moved toward the door.

"Do you mind if I clean my guns?"

Her heart gave a little skip, but of course a man on the trail would have guns for protection and hunting. "No, certainly not."

He stepped outside, picked up his rifle and his saddlebags, then sat at the table. She watched as he meticulously laid out a cloth and supplies, then pulled out his revolver, unloaded it, then took it apart, his fingers sure. Moments later the scent of gun oil filled the room as he polished every piece of the weapon.

"If you have any mending you'd like done, I wouldn't mind." She hated for her hands to be idle, but she was caught up on her sewing and was out of yarn for knitting.

He gave her a considering look. "Yeah, I'm missing a couple of buttons here and there. Sure is nice of you to have done my laundry. I can't remember the last time I had clean clothes."

She moved to his saddlebags to retrieve his clothes, since he had gun oil on his hands, but he whipped a hand out and snatched the leather pouch away from her, leaving her standing with her hands in front of her, palms out in surrender. Was he hiding something?

"I'll get it," he said, a trifle gruffly, and wiped his

hands on a rag before drawing out the damaged clothing.

She took them from him cautiously and crossed back to sit on her bed, retrieving her sewing basket on the way. Edward had occasionally behaved in such a way when there was something he didn't want her to see. What secret was Mr. Burgess keeping?

CHAPTER 3

*R*hys looked up from hitching the horse to the wagon when he heard the door close. Maddy Colby stood on the porch dressed in a fine green wool dress, a bonnet covering her red hair, her hands clasping a pocketbook in front of her.

"You going to be warm enough like that?" he asked. The wind had stopped blowing, but frost had covered everything when he woke this morning. The sun was shining now, but clouds loomed in the distance. They might be taking a bit of a risk going into town today. As he recalled it was almost an hour away.

"I have my shawl."

"Nothing heavier?"

She followed his gaze to the clouds to their north. "You think I'll need my winter coat?"

"Mrs. Colby, I need my winter coat just standing here. So, yes, ma'am, I think you should take it."

She turned back into the house. Moments later she emerged in a full-length coat with fur trim at the neck and sleeves—the first time he'd seen her with something that the Colbys' ill-gotten gains could have bought her. She fidgeted beneath his gaze.

"It's a bit fine for a ride to town."

"I found a lap robe. It will keep it clean. And the drive shouldn't be too dusty after that rain." He moved to the foot of the steps and she put her gloved hand in his. He guided her down the steps and up to the rough seat of the wagon.

She carefully smoothed out her skirt and then fidgeted with her bonnet, like she wasn't used to wearing so much.

"You doing all right?"

"I don't care for going into town."

He swung up on the seat beside her. "Why's that?"

"Too many people."

"One would think a former actress would enjoy that."

"That's not who I am anymore."

"No, you're an inventor."

She offered him a nervous smile. "I'm a woman who's looking for an easier way. My mind is always figuring things out. And I have time to indulge myself." She smoothed her hands over the pocketbook on her lap. "I don't sit still often."

"I had noticed that."

"And you know how to stay still."

"I do."

She blew out a sigh. "I wish I could."

She managed, somewhat, on the way into town. He kept an eye on her to make sure she wasn't too cold. It was hard to tell, as much as she wiggled on the seat. Her fidgeting got worse as they approached town, a single street with less than two dozen buildings lining either side, some with false fronts, some white-washed, some with raw wood.

"First stop?" he asked.

"The general store. Then the feed store. Then perhaps the butcher." When he looked at her she shrugged. "Butchering is one chore I don't care to do myself."

He drew the wagon in front of the general store, one of the older buildings, and hopped down to help her out of the wagon. She lingered on the sidewalk as he tied up the horses.

"Go inside where it's warm," he chided.

"I'm fine," she said, her teeth chattering.

He tied a blanket around the horse with a sigh, then mounted the sidewalk and took Maddy's arm to lead her inside.

A wall of warmth hit them as they entered the store and Rhys felt his body relax. Maddy, however, tensed further and turned away from the husband and wife proprietors to scurry down the crowded aisle, a basket looped over her arm. Rhys removed his hat in salute to the older woman behind the counter. The woman granted him a brief glance, but her eyes narrowed as she watched Maddy loading items in the basket. A hostility he didn't understand tightened the woman's stature, and it seemed to be directed at Maddy.

Instinctively, he moved to Maddy's side as she filled her basket with staples. She didn't skimp, didn't act like a woman on a budget as she added sugar and molasses and white flour. She moved to the back of the store to inspect the fabric. He watched her small hands caress the different textures before she set her basket down and pulled out a bolt, then another, then a third. Her shoulders squared, and then she turned toward the proprietress, her chin up.

"I'd like these measured out, please."

The woman approached stiffly and took the bolts. Maddy told her what she needed, then proceeded down the next aisle. Rhys took up the basket and followed.

When she was done, with more supplies than a single woman could use, they approached the counter. The owner eyeballed her purchases, opened a book and wrote the total down, all without speaking a word to her. Not credit, surely, because she had no income. What, then? The owner nodded at her, then she and Rhys carried her purchases to the wagon.

"Not very friendly there, are they?"

"They don't care for me."

"Why's that? You seem to give them a lot of business."

He hefted the bottles of kerosene into the back of the wagon.

She lowered her head, but he could still see the pink of her cheeks beneath the edge of her bonnet. "They know I was an actress in my past life, and they are not particular fans of the theater."

They thought she was a whore, she meant. For a moment, he wondered if that was how she paid her debts in town, with sexual favors. He couldn't picture it —or didn't care for imagining it, anyway, her pretty, lush body beneath a heaving old man. Her body was meant to be cherished, not used.

He needed to steel himself against sympathy—and lust for--this woman.

He didn't ask any more questions as they visited the feed store, where she was treated much the same, and the transaction was nearly identical to that of the general store.

"Butcher shop next?" he asked after loading bags of chicken feed and grain into the backs of the wagon. He wondered if the shop owners resented her putting so much on credit. She didn't seem to think twice about it.

She heaved a deep breath as she looked at the shop across the muddy street, then nodded.

Once he saw her safely to the butcher shop, he made an excuse of needing shaving supplies back at the general store. He needed to know what was going on here.

He was greeted with no more friendliness than

Maddy had been. He gathered what he needed, then approached the woman to complete his transaction. He saw a couple of dime novels near the counter and added them to his purchase. He didn't know if Maddy had read them or not, but they would pass the time, and keep his mind off of her.

"Will this be on Mrs. Colby's account?" the woman asked.

"No, ma'am, I have paper money." He drew out the folded bills from his back pocket.

"Are you her new man?"

"I beg your pardon?"

"I didn't figure she'd be alone long once that Colby man was killed."

"I'm doing some work around her place. She didn't mention anyone being killed."

"A bank robber, he was, and her no better, nothing more than a whore."

Rhys set his jaw. He wasn't here to defend Maddy's honor, but to find information.

"Yet you let her buy on credit?"

The woman huffed out a disgusted breath. "She's not buying on credit. The other one, Luke Colby, brother to Edward, pays her bills."

Excitement leapt in Rhys's chest. Just what he'd been hoping to hear. "Is he due to come pay her bills soon?"

"I certainly hope so. We need the money to pay our suppliers."

With that information, he walked out of the general

store and saw her huddled by the wagon, her face turned toward it.

"What is it?" he asked, touching her arm.

She shook her head, her face averted. He felt a shudder run through her and realized she was crying.

"Did something happen at the butcher shop?"

She lifted her face, blotchy with tears, her jaw gritted. "Nothing I shouldn't be used to by now."

"Do you need me to go get the purchases?"

"Would you?" Her eyes widened with gratitude. "That would be wonderful. And then we can go eat a warm lunch in the hotel."

He cast a cautious glance at the skies, the heavy gray clouds that had rolled closer. "All right. Meet me there."

MADDY SET her gloves on the tablecloth beside her plate and stroked them nervously. She'd always wanted to have lunch in the Driscoll Hotel, but never had the nerve to come alone. She looked across the table at Mr. Burgess, so handsome and strong. He'd been a great source of comfort to her during this trip, and she felt a little more confident with him by her side.

He was very quiet during their meal of warm beef stew and bread. For a moment she wondered if the Shepherds had told him tales about her. But no, he didn't seem to be overly concerned with gossip, though he glanced occasionally out the window.

"What is it?"

"I'm afraid there's going to be snow and it will be difficult to get back to the ranch."

A new tension seized her. "I need to get back. The animals need to be tended to."

"We probably should leave soon." The tightness of his jaw told her he thought even that put them at risk.

She straightened her place setting. "All right. Let's order a dinner to take with us and get started."

"We could stay in town until the worst has passed," he ventured.

She met his gaze. "No one will rent me a room, I'm sorry to say. I'm fortunate they allowed me to sit in the dining room." She looked around at the sparsely populated room. Likely that was why—they had no other business. "I'll order the food and get this packaged up. You get the horse ready."

EITHER THE TEMPERATURE had dropped when she was in the restaurant, or she was accustomed to the warmth of the building, because she started shivering the moment she stepped outside. She couldn't allow Mr. Burgess to see, or he would insist they stay in town. She would hate that.

He lifted the lap robe for her and helped her into the wagon. Warmth touched her toes as she settled in.

"I got some hot bricks from the hotel. They'll keep our feet warm for the short term, anyway." He rounded the wagon, hopped in and pulled the edge of the lap robe over his thighs.

His body heat added to the warmth from the bricks and Maddy shifted closer unconsciously. He glanced down, offered a small smile and accommodated her with a shift of his arm as he drove the horse out of town.

The snow didn't start until the town was no longer visible. It fell lightly at first, then in heavy wet clumps. Mr. Burgess set his hat farther forward on his head, and Maddy kept her face bent against the wind. The bricks had cooled rapidly, and Maddy no longer thought twice about snuggling against Mr. Burgess for warmth. He wrapped his free arm around her, drawing her closer.

"At least the meat won't go bad," she said through chattering teeth, and was rewarded by his chuckle.

She reached up to wipe frost from his whiskers with her gloved hand. "Should I drive a while?" That way he could keep both hands under the blanket for a time. Even her hands in her gloves were cold. His must feel like ice.

"I'm fine."

"Would you tell me if you weren't?" she challenged.

He grinned. "Probably not."

"I'm sure you've never been called stubborn before."

"Once or twice," he drawled.

But conversation took too much energy and she drifted against his shoulder.

He jerked beneath her. "Don't you go to sleep," he

said sternly. "If you fall asleep, I'll make you get out and walk."

For a moment her drowsy mind wondered at his change in mood, but then she remembered. Falling asleep in the cold was too dangerous.

"All right." She lifted her too-heavy head and shifted away from him. The urge to lean into him was too strong, and made her sleepy. The cool air between them made her more alert.

"Smart girl. Talk to me, now."

"'Bout what?"

"Tell me everything you want me to do to your place to fix it up."

"Hm. Would love to see it whitewashed."

"Maybe we should have bought some whitewash, then."

"Have some. In the barn."

"I'll get right on that after the snow melts."

"The fence line needs to be checked."

"I can do that. What else?"

"Probably a new door hung on the barn. I'm not strong enough to do it myself. I could help, though."

"Yes, you could."

"I wish I had insisted on a separate bedroom. I hate having my bed right next to my dining table."

"Handy when you're living alone."

"And not hard to clean."

"Was it your husband's place before you married, or did he build it for you?"

"It was his place." She shifted on the seat again. "Did they tell you in town? About him?"

"About your husband?"

"That he's gone? That he was killed robbing a bank?"

He turned his head to look at her. No surprise showed on his face. "They told me."

"I should have told you. You understand why I didn't."

"You wanted me to think you were a married woman so I would think your husband was coming home. I understand that."

"I didn't know you. I wish I'd told you myself, that you hadn't heard from someone else."

"Did you know he was a bank robber?"

She hadn't expected the question, or the way it plunged her back in time to the first time she'd seen them, Edward and Luke, so handsome, so virile, so different from the skinny actor she'd been sharing a bed with. The actor, Jeremy, had slunk away with one look from Edward. She'd fallen for him first, and agreed to let his brother join them after a few weeks. She'd delighted in the wickedness, and hadn't thought twice about what the two did for a living that made them able to indulge her every whim. "Not when I met him. He was this charming man, you know? Handsome and willing to spend money, and infatuated with me."

"And when you found out?"

She fidgeted again. She hated admitting how stupid and shallow she'd been. "I was already in love with him.

I thought it was exciting. I'd pretended to be all these things, but he was living a real adventure. I didn't think of the danger he put others in, or the harm he'd be in."

"When did he bring you to the farm?"

"There were lawmen on his trail and he feared they would use me to get to him, so he wanted me out of sight. And then I started liking being self-sufficient and he liked having me hidden away. No doubt there were other women. And then the marshal came to tell me he'd been killed." Her emotions had been all over the place as she'd looked up at the somber man who couldn't be bothered to get off his horse to deliver the news. Hurt and sorrow. Anger at Edward for getting so cocky and getting himself killed. Anger at herself for being pulled into the life of a bank robber's mistress. And an odd sense of freedom. The farm was hers now, all hers. She wasn't rich, but she owned land and a house and didn't have to answer to anyone.

"Why did you stay?"

"Where would I go? My parents wouldn't have me home, and even if they did, I'd be living by their rules, not mine. Back to the stage?" She shook her head. She'd missed the traveling and some of the companionship, but not the competition, not the constant play for her attentions. "I'm content."

"Not lonely."

"Maybe I will be by spring. Maybe I'll be crazy and scream at anyone who approaches the place. People will tell tales about the outlaw's widow who lost her mind."

She chuckled softly, picturing herself with wild hair and torn clothes, jabbering to herself.

Just then they crested the rise above the farmhouse. The scene was idyllic, snow floating around, covering everything, making it look beautiful and not run-down. Beside her, Mr. Burgess heaved a sigh of relief, and in front of them, the horse pricked up his ears and picked up the pace. Within minutes they were at the front porch. Jack crawled out from beneath it, wagging his tail anxiously.

"Start the fire while I see to the stock," he said.

"I can get the chickens."

"Don't worry about them. I'll do it. You get inside and get warm."

She walked toward the back of the wagon.

"The supplies can keep until morning."

"Our dinner," she said simply, and pulled out the basket the hotel restaurant had packed for them. "I'll get this warming." She headed toward the door, Jack on her heels.

He nodded, then drove the wagon toward the barn.

Rhys was stiff with cold when he entered the little house several long minutes later. Every chore had taken twice as long because he had trouble moving his fingers. A fire roared in the fireplace, but the heat hadn't permeated the room. She bent over the cast-iron stove, poking at another fire there, and he thought he smelled coffee. She still wore her coat, though her bonnet hung by the fire, dripping on the wood floor.

When she heard the door close, she looked up, then crossed to him, unbuttoning his coat, pushing the damp cloth from his shoulders.

"You need to get out of your wet clothes. You'll catch a chill. I can't get it warm enough in here." She crossed to hang his coat with her bonnet, then came back to him to rub at his cheeks. "Take off your boots and come to the fire. I have some wool socks you can wear."

Good, because his feet were blocks of ice inside his boots, and he fumbled to remove them. She bent quickly and urged him to lift one foot, then the other, so she could help. Before he could protest, she'd stripped off his socks, too.

She was so lovely, so sweet, so giving, so vulnerable. Every rule he'd ever followed, every rule that led his actions every day of his life, fled as he looked down at her kneeling before him.

"Your clothes are wet, too," he said when she dragged a chair from the table, placed it in front of the fire and pushed him into it.

"I didn't walk through the snow back to the house." But she did take off her coat, then shivered. "Coffee's brewing, and I'm warming our dinner. Once we get something warm inside us—"

She broke off when he caught her hand and pulled her sideways into his lap, chafing her reddened hands between his. The weight of her on his lap felt good, felt right. He had only intended to warm her, but the way she snuggled into him made him remember how long it had been since he held a woman in his arms.

"Take off your boots," he urged, his hand sliding down the front of her skirt to assist.

"I should get those wool socks," she said, a touch breathless as he lifted her foot and unlaced the boot. She shook it loose and it fell to the floor with a thump.

"I can't reach the other one," he said, and watched the skin of her throat quiver at the touch of his hot breath. What would she do when he touched her?

"I'll get it. And the socks," she said, but made no move to leave, only nestled closer. "You're warmer than I expected."

He chuckled softly as all the blood rushed from where it was needed in his extremities to the place right where her hip rested. No doubt she could feel the rise of his cock, even through the layers of her skirts.

"I have bricks warming for the bed," she murmured, turning her face toward him shyly. "No sense you sleeping on the cold floor."

Blood surged to his groin so quickly he was dizzy with it. "Mrs. Colby," he managed, sliding his hand up her thigh, over her skirts.

"Maddy," she corrected, her gaze on his mouth.

"Maddy," he repeated. "Call me Rhys."

And then, against every sense in his head, he kissed her, her cool lush lips warming quickly beneath his, parting in welcome for his tongue as his hand massaged her leg. She curved her hand behind his neck, threading her fingers through his hair as she invited a deeper kiss.

She tasted wonderful, smoky and spicy, hot and crisp, and her lips were so soft, as was the skin of her cheek as he caressed it. He'd forgotten how soft, how fragile women were. What was he doing here?

He tightened his hand on her leg and drew her closer, but not close enough. Never had desire overtaken him so quickly, not since he was an untried boy with his first woman. He had to feel her beneath him, length to length. Wrapping his arms under her, he stood, lifting her, and carried her to the bed. He lowered her there, and stood over her, waiting for her protest. Instead, she reached for him. He took her hand, pressed his mouth to her palm, and knelt beside her.

Before his good sense could return, she sat up, gripping his arm for balance while she worked the buttons of his shirt with the other.

"I've wanted to do this," she said, releasing his arm to slide her hand inside, over the hair of his chest, her fingers stroking.

He closed his eyes against the flare of lust. Never had he known a woman so bold. Again, his conscience tried to question him, but he shut it down, stripping his shirt off and lowering himself over her. She glided her hands over his shoulders and down his arms, her fingertips dancing in the ridges of muscle.

"Do you know what you're doing to me?" he asked.

Her eyelashes drifted upward, and the sultry expression in her eyes told him she knew just what. He lowered his mouth to hers. Their tongues tangled, breath mingled, and he forgot all about the cold as he inhaled her scent. She arched her back to rub her breasts against him, the wool of her dress scratchy. He eased back and looked down at the row of buttons, his desire-fogged mind unable to figure out how to work them. She laughed and began unhooking them herself. He knelt and watched the fabric fall away to reveal her lawn shift and her generous breasts. She eased up on her elbows to wriggle out of the dress and he was mesmerized by the sway of her bosom. They were works of art, full and white, with rosy nipples twisted tight. He coasted his hand down the slope of one and thumbed the tip with the pad of his thumb. Maddy gasped and pressed her breast into his palm.

"Please," she said, her voice throaty.

The chill permeated for a moment, long enough for him to reach beneath them to yank back the blankets and roll her beneath him, before he lowered his mouth and sucked her nipple into his mouth.

Her cry of delight echoed in the small room, and she wrapped her arms around his head, holding him to her. He pressed the tender bud against the roof of his mouth, then drew on it before releasing it with a pop and turning his attention to the other. She wriggled beneath him, pushing her chemise down farther.

"Let me—the dress," she murmured.

He didn't want to let her go, but neither did he want

to shove up her skirts and plow into her. She deserved better, and damn, he wanted to hold her, treat her right, feel her come, make her come.

"It's been a long time," he said when she sat up and tugged her dress free, then unfastened her petticoats, one at a time. He helped her pull them down her legs, rolled off her stockings, and then she wore only her shift. Her whole body was pink, flushed with desire, but pebbled with chills.

"Get under the blankets, Maddy."

She did, then watched as he stood and pushed his own pants down. Her lower lip dropped as she stared at his cock, curving up as if beckoning to her. She pushed back the blankets enough so he could see her peel her shift over her head, beautifully naked and waiting for him.

He slid onto the cold sheets next to her and drew the blankets over both of them before he reached for her. She squeaked when his cold hand touched her waist, but then she nestled closer, sliding her hand down his chest to close around his erection. His hips jerked toward her, sliding his cock against her smooth palm. Never had his wife touched him like that, stroked him, and he couldn't help himself from pumping into her grasp.

"Maddy, I—" With the ultimate will, he broke contact. He turned her onto her back and returned his attention to her breasts, molding them between his hands, tasting her nipples, stroking the texture of them with the tip of his tongue. He trailed his nails down her belly to stroke the curls of her womanhood, then dipping between her thighs. A moan escaped him as he found her wet for him. He teased the petals of her sex apart and teased the hard nub at the apex.

Soft pants escaped her lips as she grasped his hand, holding it to her, moving into his touch. Then she went completely still, her whimpers turning into a quiet keening, and her skin trembled. She repeated his name over and over, in rhythm with his caress.

Then she softened and he raised his head to watch her face as she came, her expression ethereal as she closed her eyes and tilted her head back, her hands falling to her sides.

She was still quivering when he shifted to kneel between her legs and pushed his cock against her slick flesh. She opened for him, so small and hot, he had to grab for every piece of restraint he had to keep from ejaculating as her sex clasped him.

"Tight. God, tight." He clenched his jaw and pushed deeper.

She let her legs fall open so his groin pressed against her pussy, and she moaned, shifting her hips up so he fit fully against her. And then he began to move. To his surprise, she locked her feet around his ass and moved into him, her rhythm erratic and needy. He tried to still her with his hands on her hips, striving for some kind of control as he drove into her hot, wet channel, but she wriggled, whimpering.

"Let me—" He tried to angle her.

"I need—" She slid her hand down his chest, her fingers playing in the curls at his groin before turning and—

His balls drew up, his lust taking over as he felt her stroke her pussy, fingers flicking fast over the swollen nub. Never had he known a woman to do that. He stilled and rose on his arms to watch her touch herself, to feel her squeeze around him. And then, with another flood of wetness that enveloped him, she came, hips pumping, fingers playing, cunt milking him. He drew back and pounded into her heat, mindless with the need to feel every inch of her.

And then, in hot pulses, he came too, the orgasm seeming to come from the back of his head to the tips of his toes, filling her with his seed, hearing her moan in approval.

He stayed deep inside for a long moment, the hot wetness still so welcoming, before he dropped to his side. On impulse, he picked up her hand from where it rested on her heaving belly, and brought it to his lips. He kissed the backs of her fingers, then one at a time, drew them into his mouth, licking her juices from her. She watched him, her eyes dark, and he waited to see regret, to feel it himself, but the feeling didn't come.

"Not precisely the way I imagined we'd warm up," she murmured.

"Really? Happened just like I dreamed."

She laughed and sat up, eyeing her clothes. "It's too cold not to get dressed," she lamented.

"Why get dressed?"

"Because there's coffee and dinner."

"We'll have it in bed. You stay here."

She opened her mouth to protest, but he covered it with a kiss. He rolled out of bed, pulled on his pants and shirt, though he didn't bother to button either. He crossed to the stove.

"Wash your hands," she called from the bed.

He looked back to see her sitting up, shoulders bare above the stacks of blankets, her hair a mess. He hadn't even bothered to take her hair down and feel it in his hands.

"I usually take more time," he said as he poured the coffee into matching tin cups, then carried one to her.

"You can take more time later."

His cock jumped at the invitation, in anticipation of devouring every inch of her lush body. He was aware his cock was making the decisions here, probably bad ones. But he couldn't help himself.

She took the coffee from him and sipped, then made a face. "A little burned."

"I can make more if you like."

She shook her head. "Maybe later."

Within a few minutes, he'd spooned up their dinner and brought it to bed, and climbed back underneath the blankets. He hadn't thought his feet could get so cold being out of bed for such a short time, and he slid them toward the warmth of Maddy's body.

She jerked her legs away with a squeak, holding her

coffee and stew up high so she didn't spill them. "Get the bricks if you want to warm your feet."

He grunted. "Don't want to get back out of bed."

She lifted her eyebrows. "Then keep your cold feet away from me."

"You were so good about warming me up before," he teased, surprising himself with his own lightheartedness. When was the last time he'd teased anyone?

"Yes, well, that was mutual," she retorted saucily.

He chuckled and dug into his stew. He'd never eaten in bed with a woman before, never even considered it. But with his feet thawed and his belly filled and warmed, he couldn't imagine himself anyplace else.

"I'll get the dishes," she said when they were done.

"You're still not dressed. I'll do it. And I'll bring the bricks this time."

The cabin hadn't warmed up much, so it must be damned cold outside. He placed the bowls and cups in the sink and rinsed them with her pump as she instructed, then collected the hot bricks she'd set by the fire, wrapped them in cloth and carried them back to jam at the foot of the bed. He climbed back in, placed his feet against the heat, and found his arms full of luscious woman.

"Did the meal restore your strength?" she asked with a bat of her eyelashes.

His cock had been half-hard since their meal. "I believe it did."

She gripped the opening of his shirt and pushed it down his shoulders. "Good."

She captured his mouth with hers and lifted herself over him, pushing him back on the bed.

"One thing," he managed, and reached up to pull the pins from her hair, tossing them to the floor beside the bed. Her hair fell in a heavy mass around her shoulders, the deep color contrasting with her pale skin. He threaded his fingers through it, the calluses of his hands snagging on the silky waves.

She allowed his attention for a short time before she bent to brush kisses along his jaw, then his throat.

"So rough," she murmured.

"I bought shaving supplies." Her bare pussy rested over the open fly of his pants, and he wanted to push up, push into her, but she seemed to have an agenda.

"Doesn't matter. I like it." She nipped the flesh of his throat with her teeth, then continued downward, fingers spearing through the hair of his chest, rubbing up and down.

He watched her face as she moved to touch his nipple with her tongue, and he flinched at the strange sensation. Did it feel like that for her? But she didn't linger, her hair trailing across his chest as she kissed his belly. Her breast brushed against his erection, now painfully hard, and when he gasped, she shifted so his cock rode in the cleft between her breasts. She looked up at him, eyes dancing wickedly, and pressed a kiss to his navel.

"Maddy," he managed, then his mind went blank as she opened her mouth over the head of his cock and drew him deep. He was awash with sensation as her tongue glided down the underside of his length, as her lips closed softly around his girth, sucking gently. She lowered her head and he watched more of his cock disappear between those pretty lips. Her eyes drifted closed as if she was savoring the tastiest of treats. She rose to circle her tongue around the rim of his cock, teasing the tender flesh at the base of the head before she took him deeper. The tip of his penis tapped the back of her throat. She hummed a breath around him, then he pressed farther into her mouth, into her throat, and her lips closed around the base of him, her fingers cupping his balls.

He shouted her name again, his hand tangling in the hair at the back of her head as he struggled not to pump into her mouth.

Slowly she lifted her head, dragging her lips and tongue along his length as she did so.

"Do you want me to finish?" she asked, her voice sultry, her hair pooled in his lap, her lips swollen with her ministrations.

Knowing it was selfish, but needing to know what it would be like to come in her mouth, he nodded shortly. She smiled and settled between his legs so her breasts rubbed his thighs. She lifted his balls in her hand and gave them long, suckling kisses before she turned her attention back to his aching cock. She held his gaze as she nibbled on the tender head, then laved it with her tongue. Her eyes drifted shut again as she closed her mouth around him and did her damnedest to swallow him, tongue working, the muscles of her throat clasping. God, so wet, so hot, so erotic.

The orgasm had him trembling beneath her before his balls contracted and he erupted in her mouth. With her hands and lips she pumped his cock until every last drop was gone. Then she rested her cheek on his thigh and looked up at him, her eyes still dark with desire.

"That was—thank you," he managed.

She pushed herself up the bed to lie beside him, and brought his hand to her breast. He thumbed her nipple to a peak and she murmured her approval, then shifted, offering her breast to his mouth. He took the invitation, drawing the tender flesh between his lips. She pushed closer, and he opened his mouth wider, taking more of her in, sucking harder until she moaned her approval. Then she took his hand and placed it over her cunt.

Christ, she was wet, aroused from his own pleasure. He wished he could recover enough to plunge deep inside her, but instead he slipped his finger into her, one, then two, then three, sliding in and out, stretching her. Her hand moved from the back of his to her pussy, stroking above her opening, working the little nub, each caress making her channel wetter and wetter, until her juices coated his hand. Her muscles fluttered around his knuckles, then closed on him as her hips bucked on the bed, bringing his fingers deeper, grinding against him as she keened her pleasure.

Her hand fell to the mattress and he slid his fingers from her body to fold them through hers, and he stretched out beside her on the bed. She laughed and lifted her free hand to stroke his hair from his face. She cupped his cheek and kissed him, then turned into him and promptly fell asleep.

CHAPTER 4

Maddy stretched out on the bed, twinges reminding her of the decadent way she and Rhys had warmed up after their trip into town. She should feel ashamed, should be guilty for reveling in his touch, in his kisses, in his lovemaking.

She reached across the bed, then lifted her head when she felt the coolness of the sheets. The cabin was brighter, but the day was overcast. And Rhys was nowhere in sight. The fire burned brightly in the hearth, and she could see the stove was lit. She found her shift and dress in the tangle of blankets—had he added more overnight? She dressed as well as she could under the covers, then slipped out of bed. She looked out the window but didn't see him, but he was likely seeing to the animals.

She'd make a good breakfast, though the hour was late.

The door opened while she was making the coffee, and she turned to watch him kick the snow off his boots, and hang his hat and coat by the door. He looked at the made bed and turned to the kitchen. A blush heated his cheeks before he gave her a shy smile.

"Snow stopped but it's damned cold out there."

"Coffee will be ready soon, and I'm making eggs and sausage. It won't take long."

He nodded and crowded into the kitchen with her, wrapping his arms around her waist from behind, pressing his cold nose into the side of her neck. She squealed and laughed, then turned into his arms and folded her arms around his neck. His lips were cold, but she warmed them quickly. She couldn't believe she could heat up again so soon after last night, but when he drew her hips against his, arousal slid through her blood.

She drew back reluctantly. "You need your strength. Let me finish breakfast."

After breakfast, she felt uneasy with him for the first time since she'd met him. The kitchen was clean, the food put away, and all she could think about was the bed.

He crossed the room to a package she hadn't seen him bring in.

"I bought some books. I thought maybe we could read to each other. I wasn't sure if you'd read these, but-
-"

She gripped his hand that held the two slim novels

and read the titles. "I've read this one, but the other is new."

"Let's get under the blankets."

"I have bricks by the fireplace," she said, moving to retrieve them.

Moments later they were snuggled together under the blankets and the book was open in her hand. She was nervous reading to him, and was grateful when the chapter was over and she could hand the book over. He stumbled over the first few words and she wondered if he was nervous, too, but then he settled into a rhythm and she settled in next to him, letting his deep voice reverberate against her ear.

RHYS TUCKED the book aside and stroked the hair from Maddy's face as she slept on his chest. She looked so peaceful and sweet. Guilt clutched at his chest. He should never have taken her to bed. He was here to do a job, not to seduce her, and he'd forgotten that. Twice. Even now his cock stirred. He couldn't listen to it. He had to remember why he was here. She was a means to an end, not a means to ease his libido.

He'd never been completely ruled by his lust. There was always tenderness with every woman he'd bedded, and damned if he wasn't feeling that tenderness now. He had to put some distance between them. She had been an outlaw's mistress, but from what he could see, she had broken no laws. She didn't deserve to be hurt, and she would be, when she learned who he was and why he was here.

He could tell her who he was and why he was here, and hope she didn't kick him the hell out. But he couldn't risk that. He needed to wait for Luke. He should be along soon, and Rhys would reveal himself, get his man, and be on his way.

He hated being cut off from the rest of the service, not knowing what was going on in the manhunt. He held out hope that someone else would round up Luke Colby, and Rhys would be free to ride off into the sunset. Maddy would never have to know the truth.

No, that was the coward's way out. He couldn't do that to her. But as soon as the weather warmed up, he needed to go back to sleeping in the barn and just be her hired man. That would make it easier for them both when the time came for him to leave.

He eased from beneath her, careful not to wake her, and slipped outside, hoping the cold air would cool his desire.

The blanket of clouds was breaking up and the sun was peeking through. Snow melted in patches where the sunbeams hit, but a clear sky meant a cold night. He wondered if the weather would bounce back. Hard to believe he'd been sweating on the roof just a few days ago.

He could manage sleeping in the barn—he'd slept in worse. But the idea of leaving Maddy's bed just yet made him ache. One more night.

. . .

RHYS WAS QUIET DURING DINNER. Not that he was usually talkative, but Maddy once again felt uncomfortable with his silence. He'd tended the animals and unloaded the wagon of the supplies, then had come in to warm up, but had shown no particular affection to her. She didn't know why that should bother her. Edward had never shown her much. But in the beginning, he hadn't been able to get enough of her.

Rhys barely looked at her as he ate, but ate everything.

"Is anything wrong?" she asked, unable to bear the silence any longer.

"Not a thing. Just enjoying the good dinner."

But he hadn't said much since he came back in as she was waking from her nap. "You have a very nice voice."

He looked up at her then, eyebrows lifted in question.

She felt her cheeks heat. "I fell asleep when you were reading because it was so soothing."

He chuckled softly. "I've been told I read too slow. Glad to know the reason you fell asleep wasn't because you got tired of waiting for me to get to the next word."

"No!" But she realized he was teasing her and relaxed a little. She stood to clear the table. "I believe I would like a bath tonight."

His expression sunk into a frown. "Isn't it a bit cold for a bath? You could catch a chill."

"It's warm enough in here, and I have a big kettle to warm the water."

He shook his head. "Doesn't seem wise to me."

"I smell like smoke."

"You will again after you take the bath," he pointed out. "With a wood stove and a fireplace."

He was right, she knew, but felt sticky from their lovemaking. She could take a whore's bath, she supposed, and had done on days when she couldn't get to her shower, but tonight she didn't feel it would be enough.

"I can empty the tub myself," she said. "I just carry a bucket at a time to the sink."

"I'll get the tub," he said with a sigh, heaving to his feet.

"It's on the front porch," she said as he moved toward the door.

"I know. I've seen it." He didn't put on his coat and was back in a matter of minutes, setting the copper tub in front of the fireplace.

She gave him a grateful smile and turned to begin heating up the water.

When finally the tub was filled and steaming with hot water, Maddy stood before it, suddenly shy. He had seen her naked, had been inside her body, but this was different. She'd never bathed in front of a man before.

"Would you like me to go into the barn?" he asked. "Or move the screen?"

That would be silly, as intimate as they'd been. She

shook her head and reached for the buttons on her bodice. "Would you help me wash my hair? You'll need a pitcher."

He swallowed, then nodded, turning away as she undressed. The room was colder than she expected, without her layers of clothes, and she stepped into the tub.

The water was hot, and she squealed a bit and grabbed Rhys's arm when he moved close. She gasped at the friction of his homespun shirt against her nipples, and her eyes flashed to his. His breathing shifted at the contact, and his gaze drifted to her breasts, but then he steadied her and stepped back.

"Too cold?" he asked.

"Too hot!"

He walked to the pump, filled a bucket with water and carried it over to pour into the tub. It swirled into the hot water, leaving ribbons of iciness in its path, then it all melded into a perfect temperature. She sank into the water gratefully. Bliss—the warmth seeped into her skin, sluiced over her. Already she felt cleaner.

"I've never washed a woman's hair before," he said, pulling his chair beside the tub. "How do we go about this?"

"You pour the water over my hair, I'll soap it. The hard part is getting the soap out." She drew her braid around to unplait it. "Do you think you can help me braid it when we're done?"

He choked a little. "I would not have any idea how to do that."

"That's fine. We'll get this done first." She tilted her head back and closed her eyes. "You may wet my hair."

He hesitated a moment, and she opened her eyes to see him staring at her breasts. On impulse, she caught one of his hands and curved it over her wet skin, pushing the flesh into his palm. He stroked for a moment, his rough hand circling, before he cleared his throat and removed his touch. Maddy shifted her legs under the water against the sudden ache of arousal his caress awoke.

He poured the water then, carefully, his fingers working through the strands of her hair to make sure it was wet.

"Want me to soap it?"

The roughness of his voice told her he was affected, too. Lord, how she wished this tub was big enough for two. She'd seen such a thing in the city, in hotels, but thought of all the work it would take to fill it and empty it. At the moment, she wouldn't mind that work a bit, if it meant Rhys's naked body sliding against hers.

She nodded in answer to the question she'd almost forgotten he'd asked, and handed him the soap. Attuned to every movement now, she heard him lather it in his hands, and then his fingers were in her hair again, gently stroking, massaging, threading their way through her tresses. She moaned her pleasure at the sensation, and he gave a choked breath.

"Are you sure you've never done this before?" she prodded.

"Never."

His fingers worked the soap in so well across her scalp, she feared they'd never get it out. But she had no intention of complaining.

When he finally removed his touch, she opened her eyes to look at him. Again, his gaze was on her pebbled nipples. She wished more than anything he would kiss them, even arched her back in invitation, but he reached for the pitcher instead.

"I need to refill this," he said, and stumbled out of the chair toward the stove, where another pot of water was warming.

When he returned, she closed her eyes, bracing herself for the rinsing water. Instead, she felt a sudden heat across her body, and then his lips were on hers. Before she could do more than tilt her chin up to accept the kiss, he broke it, then shifted to smooth her hair back before pouring the water through her hair.

She could feel the change in his breathing, but he didn't say anything, only worked his fingers through her hair rinsing the soap so bubbles frothed around her. She luxuriated in the feeling of his hands in her hair, then he stopped.

"I think I got it all," he murmured.

"Can you hand me that drying sheet? I can blot the water from it with that." She pointed to the end of the bed. So strange, his reaction. He touched her, kissed her, then acted so distant.

He passed her the drying sheet and she folded it around her hair, letting it absorb as much water as it could before she hung it over the side of the tub and began to plait it—not an easy task.

Rhys knelt beside the tub and took the three strands. "Tell me what to do."

"Cross the right hand section over the middle section. Make sure it's tight."

"Maddy, you're going to get cold with this hair."

"I'll be fine. Did you do it?"

"Yes, ma'am."

"Now take the left hand section and cross it over the middle section, then pull it tight."

He did, and she only had to give directions twice more before his sure fingers finished the job faster than she could have done. He let the end of the braid hang over the edge of the tub and rose.

"Is the water still warm?"

"It feels lovely."

She picked up the soap and lathered her arms, then her breasts. A muffled groan from Rhys told her he was watching, and suddenly her bath became something else, a seduction. She lingered with her hands on her breasts, then slid her left hand beneath the water, over her belly, to bathe the folds between her legs. She rubbed back and forth, then raised one leg out of the water to stroke the bar of soap along its length, bending forward to lather her toes before dunking them, then lifting her right leg out of the water, straight up, to bathe it. When Rhys coughed, she smiled over her shoulder at him. He sat on the bed, riveted by her ministrations, his hand high on his thigh. Had he been touching himself?

"Would you mind scrubbing my back?"

He hesitated, then knelt behind her. She handed the soap and washcloth over her shoulder. He took the soap and draped the washcloth over the edge. Once again she heard him lather the soap between his hands, the scent of lavender filling the air.

Then his fingers were on her skin, on her shoulders, rubbing, then sliding down to the waterline and below before trailing up along her spine. Everything female in her responded to the slow, leisurely caresses. Her breasts ached for his touch, her thighs quivered, wanting to spread for his touch, for his cock. She dipped her shoulders below the water to rinse the soap from her skin before she rose on her knees, hooked her hand around the back of his neck and kissed him.

He closed his hands around her waist and stood, hauling her to her feet and out of the tub in the same movement. He wrapped another drying sheet around her, then lowered her to the rug by the fire, following her down. She opened her legs for him, wanting to feel the roughness of his trousers against her inner thighs, wanting to feel his arousal pulse against her sex.

He held his weight off of her the best he could, so she wrapped her legs around his hips, urging him over her.

Her nipples rasped against the drying sheet, but she wanted to feel the roughness of his shirt, followed by the heat of his mouth. Her swollen folds rubbed against the cotton, but she wanted to feel the tickle of his body hair. She released her grip on the back of his neck and moved her hand between them to unbutton his shirt. She wriggled so the drying sheet came loose and she could press her breasts against the hair of his chest.

"Maddy," he said against her mouth, almost a protest, but her hand slipped deeper to close around his cock through the thick wool of his trousers.

"Fill me up, Rhys. I need you to fill me up."

He sat up, breaking the kiss and her grip on his manhood. Just when she thought he might turn away, he parted the sheet and thrust his fingers between her legs. She moaned, tilting her head back and pumping against his invasion. He wasn't filling her the way she wanted, but the sensation was exquisite nonetheless, his big fingers sliding in and out of her, spreading her cream over her folds, his thumb circling her swollen flesh, the part of her womanhood that she often caressed to bring herself to pleasure.

And then…then he lowered his mouth to it. With the gentlest of kisses, he nibbled at the sensitive nub before stroking his tongue over it, his caresses in time with the thrusts of his fingers. Higher and higher he pushed her, tongue and fingers, the roughness of his beard against the inside of her thighs, a gentle caress of his free hand up and down her leg, until she was nothing but sensation, nothing but pleasure and anticipation and desire in one glorious ball of light.

His tongue stroked just so and she flew apart, the orgasm shooting through her blood, her hips lifting against his mouth to prolong the feeling, her hands falling to her sides helplessly as she rode it out.

And then he was over her, his lips seeking hers. She turned her face toward him, accepting the kiss that felt so wicked, his lips wet with her cream. Shyly she touched her lips to his, then slipped her tongue out to taste herself on his skin. Salty, not unpleasant, and her willingness seemed to please him, so she licked more, as he pressed the head of his cock against her entrance and slid slowly into her still-clutching channel. He reached behind her and pressing his hand into the small of her back, lifting her into him, thrusting gently, urging her response. She dug her heels into the rug beneath her for purchase and matched him stroke for stroke, loving the feel of his body grinding against hers when they met, loving the stretch of him deep inside her, taking a breath in anticipation every time he withdrew, almost completely.

She gasped when his thrusts grew a little rougher, his body slamming against her tender folds with greater force.

"Did I hurt you?" he asked against her ear.

"More," she demanded, parting her legs wider, allowing him greater movement, allowing herself the ability to lift into him. She grew wetter with each collision of their bodies, that little nub that had so much recent attention swelling again with each thrust.

He gripped her hips in his hands and pounded into her. Her body wept, easing his strokes. His skin slickened with sweat as he powered over her, into her, and she tried to match him, to find the release he offered but that was just out of reach. Still, the way his cock filled her, over and over, stroking along every nerve inside her, making her wetter and wetter, making her swell for him, squeeze him—

She couldn't help herself. She slid her hand between them and stroked over the needy bundle of flesh, circling, flicking, finding.

Heat raced along her skin as her cunt closed around him, gripping, holding, until she could feel everything, every vein in his cock, every ripple of her own sex, falling in on herself instead of flying apart. The spasms were long and hard, and she rocked against him in time to them as he stilled with a shout and poured into her in hot spasms.

He held himself over her for a long time before he tumbled onto his side, keeping her closer to the fire, his fingers trailing over her breasts and stomach and hip. When she looked up at him, his eyes were closed, and a smile canted his lips.

"Now I need a bath," he teased.

.   .   .

THEY WASHED up in the lukewarm water and he bundled her into bed, where he should have taken her in the first place. He was worried she'd get a chill, and what had he done? Plowed her in front of the fireplace. Not very well done of him. He hadn't thought twice about his vow to keep his distance from her. But now he had her in a woolen nightgown, her hair wound at the back of her head, the bricks at the foot of the bed, and his arms around her. One last night. Tomorrow he'd go back to the barn, back to the place he'd made for himself, and shut down all the feelings he had toward her that he couldn't afford to indulge.

But at some point in the night, she reached for him, her hands soft, her lips eager. She slipped her hand into his long johns and stroked him until he was hard—which took about half a minute. She rose over him, the heavy braid falling over one shoulder, her breasts peeking out through the opening in her gown, and she took him into her heat.

"How are you so wet?" he asked through his teeth, finding her naked hips under the voluminous skirt.

"Dreaming about you." She captured his hands and brought them to her breasts, squeezing as she moved up and down on his cock, her movements erratic so that he thought he'd slide free. "I need your mouth."

With a groan, he curled upward, pulling his hand free and baring her breast for his mouth. Her fingers dug into the back of his scalp as he suckled hard.

He'd never known a woman like her, one who was so

independent, who knew what she wanted, in bed and out. He'd never experienced sex when he was barely awake and it was all sensation and desire.

She guided his head to her other breast. He shoved her braid out of the way and curved his hand underneath to lift the heavy globe, stroking his thumb over the underside. Her pussy bathed his cock until all he could think of was her tight, wet channel. He tried to lift into her but had no leverage. He dragged her hips closer and bent his legs behind her but even then his movements were frustrated.

He released her breast and lay back, hands on her hips as he pounded into her, struggling to match her rhythm, unable to, but driving her to a quivering mass. The muscles of her thighs trembled, her inner core rippled. And then she let go with a cry, her body arched, her braid brushing the top of his legs, and he jerked as the orgasm ripped through him, pouring him into her.

When she'd fallen back to sleep beside him, he laid in the dark and wondered how the hell he'd let himself fall in love with her.

He had to tell her the truth.

THE NEXT DAY was much warmer. In typical Texas fashion, the temperatures were downright springlike. The snow had melted, making the yard muddy, but that didn't keep Maddy inside. As Rhys worked on the chicken coop, he watched as Maddy stopped hanging laundry to play with Jack in the yard, her hair loose about her face.

She tossed her hair and looked up at him with that brilliant smile. It hit him in the gut, followed by that stab of guilt. He'd tell her the truth tonight and hope that she understood his objective enough to overlook his lies. She'd been an actress after all. She knew the importance of keeping in character.

Who was he kidding? She was going to be furious, and hurt.

As much as he hated the thought, he had to do it. He'd started earlier, during breakfast, but the words stuck in his throat. He told himself he was worried about losing ground on finding Luke Colby, but now he knew he couldn't go one more day without telling her.

He climbed down the ladder and crossed the yard. She tugged the stick from Jack's mouth and straightened with a smile.

"I was thinking if the weather stays nice we can go to town tomorrow."

"Why?" he asked, taken aback. They'd gone just three days ago.

"I want to get more of the sausage before winter sets in."

"All the way to town for sausage?"

"I'm not likely to get it for a while."

Pure fear shot through him. He'd heard of women having cravings when they were with child. She could be pregnant, something he hadn't considered when he'd emptied his seed inside her again and again. He and Polly hadn't had any children, so he hadn't considered. But now…

Even if these weren't those kinds of cravings, it didn't mean she wasn't pregnant. She wouldn't know right away, would she? She might find out long after he was gone. He lifted his hand to his face and rubbed.

"We need to talk."

She cocked her head and a slight frown marred the smooth skin of her forehead. "All right. I have another batch of clothes on the stove. As soon as I'm done with that, all right?"

He rocked back on his heels. He wanted her undivided attention, so, yes, he'd wait. He helped her pin the remaining laundry on the line, then she hurried into the house.

* * *

MADDY HAULED the sheets out of the pot and into the sink. She'd let it drain a bit and put another load in. She wondered if Rhys had anything she needed to wash. She'd only seen him in two shirts. Surely he had more, and if he didn't, maybe she could use the fabric she'd bought and make him one. She could use buttons from one of Edward's old shirts. She'd just make a pattern out of one of Rhys's shirts. While she waited for the laundry to cool off enough to handle, she picked up his bags.

After just a moment of wondering if she might be over-stepping her bounds, she reached inside.

Her fingers brushed something cold and round. She closed her fingers around it, her thumb brushing the surface. She knew what it was before she saw it laying in her palm.

A silver marshal's star.

Maddy could hardly catch all the thoughts racing through her head. Had he killed a marshal and taken his badge?

That her first thought painted him as an outlaw alarmed her. But the only other option was that he was a marshal and he'd lied to her. Her whole body ran cold at the thought. These past few nights in his arms—the way he'd looked at her, the way he'd touched her so reverently. Had anything this week been real?

She jolted when Jack started barking, sharp and alarmed. She almost dropped the badge, then tightened her fingers around it, rising to look out the window. Before she had a chance to do more than count two riders approaching, three steps reverberated on the porch and the door swung in.

Her whole body tensed when Rhys stopped, facing her, his eyes traveling from his bag at her feet to the star clutched in her hand. His jaw clenched, and when he met her gaze, real regret flashed in his eyes.

"Luke Colby is here."

Luke. Her knees wobbled. That was why Rhys was here. Her suspicion was confirmed when he grabbed his six-shooter from its holster by the door. He lowered it to his thigh and stepped outside.

"Stay inside, away from the window."

"Are you going to shoot him?" The shrillness of her voice startled them both.

His mouth formed a grim line as he reached for the door handle. "If it comes to that." He closed the door behind him.

RHYS'S FINGERS flexed on the grip of his pistol as he stayed in the shadows of the porch. Of all the damn times for Luke to show up, for Maddy to be nosing around in his things. Christ. But he couldn't let concern for anything but her safety cloud his thoughts. He took in the two riders approaching down the hill, Luke Colby on the paint, and who he suspected was Tim Givens on the roan.

"Put my rifle by the door," he said through the door, and hoped she could hear him over the barking dog, hoped she would do it. The way she'd looked when he walked in, pale with shock, he wasn't sure she'd respond. He couldn't be sure she didn't want him dead.

Luke pulled his horse up into the yard. Jack, losing

his mind on the porch, made the roan toss his head and shy away from the porch, so Tim Givens guided his mount to the center of the yard. Luke tilted his hat back to look at Rhys.

"Marshal."

"Colby."

"Been waiting here long?"

"Few days. Snow slow you down?"

"Not as much as the whores in Fort Worth."

Colby flashed a grin that might be considered charming. He knew it had worked on Maddy. He shook off the thought. He couldn't let himself think of her now.

"So what's going to happen now, Marshal? You going to shoot me?"

"I'd like to take you in alive."

"I don't intend to go peacefully. And my man Tim there?" Colby inclined his head toward the other outlaw, who had calmed his mount and was sitting completely still, his rifle leveled over his pommel, aimed at Rhys.

Colby hadn't cleared his holster but Rhys knew well enough that he could draw before Rhys could put Givens down. Shit. He didn't want Maddy to see him killed.

Didn't want her to see anyone killed. But he didn't see a way out of this without violence.

Shit. He hoped she listened to him and stayed down.

"Luke."

All of the blood rushed out of his head when the

door swung open and Maddy stepped out. Only his years of experience kept him from pivoting toward her.

"Jesus, Maddy. Get back inside," he said through his teeth.

"Maddy," Luke drawled, still making no move for his gun. "Helping the marshal with his little ambush."

The sound of a load racking in a shotgun echoed across the yard. Holy hell. Maddy had his shotgun, and she could barely hold the rifle she'd greeted him with. Rhys eased back so he could keep his attention on the outlaws and still disarm Maddy, who pointed the shotgun at Luke.

She may be pissed off at Rhys but at least she wasn't aiming at him.

"Put the gun down, Maddy."

"No. It's two to one. I'm evening the odds. Then you can all get the hell off my land."

Tension thickened the air, and his gut tightened. He couldn't keep track of all three. Every instinct told him Givens was waiting for an opportunity to fire. When he did, Colby would draw. Rhys hoped he'd fire at him, and not Maddy. Rhys played everything out in his head, as he always did, accounting for the variables. Maddy being one of the variables, he also prayed.

Then, everything happened at once. Maddy shifted the weight of the gun. Givens fired, either threatened by the move or taking advantage of Rhys's momentary distraction. The post inches from Rhys's head exploded in splinters. Rhys launched himself sideways, knocking

Maddy to the porch as his finger reflexively pulled the trigger.

Givens dropped out of the saddle, a hole between his eyes. Even as Rhys registered that, another shot rang out. Beneath him, Maddy cried out in pain. Rhys had to shut that out as he focused on Colby. He trained his gun on Luke, who fired another shot. Rage tried to overtake reason, but he couldn't kill the outlaw. He fired, putting a bullet through Luke's gun hand. Colby's pistol went flying, and he grabbed his wrist, staring at his ruined hand.

But he still sat astride his horse, and if he thought past the pain another moment, he'd take off. Even as Rhys listened to Maddy's labored breathing beneath him, he made a choice and shot the man in the leg. Colby dropped out of the saddle. Rhys pushed himself off Maddy and crossed the yard. He scooped up Colby's gun, then looked down at the bleeding, wounded man. He frisked the outlaw and collected two more guns and a knife, then slammed the butt of his gun against Colby's skull. The outlaw fell into the mud.

Only then could Rhys return to the porch and drop to his knees beside Maddy. She stared up at him, sweating and pale.

"Where?" he asked, but her lips only parted on shallow breaths.

His gaze locked on the blood blooming on her shoulder. He reached beneath her skirt to rip her petticoat.

He wadded the soft cotton and pressed it to her wound. She barely managed a mewl of pain.

He needed to assess the damage. Had the bullet gone through, or was it lodged inside her? A steady stream of curses poured from his lips as he ripped her blouse open. He'd seen blood plenty in his line of work, but seeing it welling from a bullet hole in the woman he loved made him want to retch. But he couldn't allow himself the luxury. He was her only help.

Holding the torn petticoat against the hole in her skin, he eased her onto her uninjured arm to look at her back, searching for an exit wound.

He didn't know whether or not to be relieved that it hadn't exploded through her shoulder. No, the damned ball was stuck inside her and he had to get it out before he stopped the bleeding with stitches.

"Are you hurt anywhere else?" he asked, remembering that second shot. He lowered her onto her back and looked at her face, but she only blinked at him. Blood covered her breast. He couldn't delay. He drew out his knife and sliced her blouse and skirt. He inspected her pale, clammy skin, but saw no other injuries. Thank God.

Her eyes drifted shut and panic squeezed his chest. Was she losing consciousness?

Rhys sat on his heels and considered his options. He could move her to the bed and try to get the ball out himself, hoping he didn't cause too much damage, or hook up the team, get her in the wagon and haul her over the hills and into town.

No, he was going to have to stop the bleeding. He scooped her into his arms and shoved the door open with his shoulder. The scrabble of the dog's nails on the floor drew his attention and he looked into Jack's eyes. The animal's eyebrows were drawn together as if in concern. If only the damned dog could help him.

Damn it, he needed Luke's help. He hated even considering it, but he had no choice. Once he insured that Maddy was as comfortable as he could make her, he strode across the yard and dragged Colby up by his good arm.

The outlaw's hand was a mess, missing two fingers, and he was pale and sweaty himself. But he'd shot Maddy and he'd help her before he got attention himself.

When he prodded Colby into the room ahead of him, the first thing he noticed was that Maddy wasn't passed out as he'd thought. Eyes swimming with tears of pain, she watched them from the bed, her hand pressing the bloody cloth to her shoulder. Her breathing seemed to have evened out, seemed less panicked.

"Rhys," she said.

"I'll get you fixed up," he promised, prompting Colby into a chair. He needed to give the man some cursory medical attention so the outlaw didn't pass out while he was helping.

He used Maddy's ruined dress as a tourniquet for

Colby's wounds. The bullet had passed through the meaty part of Colby's lower leg, and the bleeding was sluggish, but Rhys tied it off anyway.

"I have whiskey in my saddlebag. For the pain," Colby said.

"Yours or hers?" Rhys muttered.

"Mostly mine, but she can have some, too, if she needs it."

Rhys went outside to retrieve the saddlebag from the skittish horse, then all but ran inside. Once Colby had drunk what he needed, Rhys hauled him to his feet.

"Now. You hold her down while I get the bullet out."

THE NEXT HOUR passed the slowest of any in Rhys's life, and he'd spent days on surveillance. Digging into Maddy's soft skin with his knife until she passed out from the pain, pulling out a bullet, depending on Colby's help as he stitched her up the best he could.

"I never would have thought she'd turn a gun on me," Colby muttered, pinching her skin closed as Rhys pushed the needle through it.

"Maybe she got tired of being all alone out here in a house with a leaking roof."

"She knows she could hire anyone in town to do it."

"She doesn't like the way they look at her, knowing what she was to you and your brother. She doesn't like to go to town."

Colby sat back, releasing Maddy's skin. "Well, hell, Marshal, did you go and fall in love with our girl, here?"

Rhys pressed his lips together as he continued to stitch.

"My little Maddy, in love with a lawman. Never thought that would happen. But she came to your rescue."

Rhys did not want to discuss this with the outlaw, but apparently pain and whiskey loosened Colby's tongue.

"You screwed her, I know you did. I can smell you on her bed. Thought you were tougher than that, Marshal, falling for a pretty face."

"I'm not the one she turned the gun on," Rhys muttered.

"I didn't mean to shoot her."

"Of course not. She just got in the way of your bullet."

"Meant for you. Hell, if I'd known you were screwing her, I'd have taken more time with my aim."

Rhys bared his teeth at the other man, then finished off the stitches and punched Colby in the injured leg with all his strength. The other man howled and passed out.

<h1 style="text-align:center">CHAPTER 6</h1>

Maddy cradled her arm as she looked out the second story window at the town below. People hurried place to place, heads bent against the wind. The spring temperatures hadn't lasted long, but at least this new storm didn't bring snow.

She was warm and well-fed—and alone.

She turned from the window and adjusted the sling holding her arm immobile. She'd woken up two weeks ago to learn that Rhys had brought her here, paid for the room and a doctor, and left.

She shouldn't expect anything more from the man who'd come into her life, charmed her, made love to her, all while he lied about who he was. How had she let herself be fooled? Because she was lonely and he was handsome and kind and—and lying to her. Using her. No better than Luke and Edward had done. Worse, because he was the law.

She'd replayed everything in her mind, looking for clues, and could find none. Not in the way he talked to her, or touched her, or kissed her. Perhaps he didn't come to her thinking to bed her, but she felt used all the same.

Now it was time to go home. She'd have to hire someone to drive her because she couldn't manage her wagon, though she'd been told it was waiting for her at the livery, also paid for by Rhys. But she needed to get home to Jack and her chickens and her cows and her life. Funny how she never felt as lonely as she did when she was in town.

"No, ma'am, I don't know anyone who can drive you home today," the proprietor Mr. Ackles told her, his hands braced on the counter in front of him as if to hold himself as far away from her soiled reputation as possible. "The weather is downright raw, and I don't know anyone who would venture out in it on purpose. Your room here is paid another week. Why don't you wait for a more suitable travel day?"

"I'll pay whoever takes me home. I have responsibilities there." And the peace to nurse a broken heart.

"The marshal said we were to take good care of you. Are we not? You won't be able to manage on your own with your injury." Curiosity about her wound brightened his eyes.

No doubt he knew she'd been shot, but she

wondered if he knew the details. She certainly had no intention of telling him. "When do you think it might be possible?"

"Another day or so. Would you like me to send dinner to your room?"

He'd been doing that to keep her away from the respectable citizens of town. But since he was unwilling to help her…

"I believe I'll take dinner in the dining room today. I would like a seat by the window. In fact, I believe I'll take every meal in the dining room until I go home. Would you please send up a maid to help me with my hair?"

One of the more frustrating things about her injury was being unable to wash her own hair. She worked past the pain to button her blouse, well, after the first week, when she wore nothing but her nightgown. But she couldn't lift her arm long enough to wash or pin up her hair.

"Could you send up a basin and warm water and soap, too, please? And scissors." Even if she had to cut it to her scalp, she was going to have clean hair.

Mr. Ackles looked askance, then nodded.

MADDY FELT ALMOST human as she made her way to the dining room a few hours later. She was bathed, and with the maid's help, had cut her hair to her shoulders, a manageable length with her injury. Seeing the lengths of tresses on the floor had saddened her for a moment, but this was more practical. And pretty, if she allowed herself that. Her hair had bounced back in cunning little waves. She drew attention as she walked through the door, and not the recoiling kind. No, she received some admiring glances, which served her battered heart well. She took her seat by the window and ordered soup, something she could easily eat with one hand. She didn't like being in the middle of town, sitting in the window on display, but she had a point to make. She wanted to go home.

The low clouds added to the chill she felt through the glass. Possibly she should have asked to sit closer to the fire, but no, this was what she needed to do. She ate slowly, though her nervousness made her want to rush and retreat. When she was done, she asked for coffee and a slice of pie, which was really delicious. She never made pies for herself because she could never eat the whole thing.

Full and satisfied, she left the dining room for the stairs.

And stopped still when she saw a lean figure near the check-in counter. She knew that coat, that hat, those mannerisms.

Mr. Ackles looked past Rhys to her. "Wouldn't you like to stay in Mrs. Colby's room? You're already paying for it."

"I don't think Mrs. Colby would be very welcoming," Rhys said with a heavy sigh.

"And you'd be right about that," she couldn't stop herself from saying.

He turned and her heart jumped when his gaze met hers, bright with an emotion she chose not to name. She took a step back when he moved forward, his hand extended. She bit back all the accusations, swallowed all the pain at being abandoned here.

He lowered his hand, his expression collapsing into a frown. "You look well."

She tightened her injured arm against her waist. "I'm going home tomorrow."

"I've come to take you back."

"You can go to hell."

"Hey, now," Mr. Ackles said, stepping from around the counter.

"Let's go to your room. We can talk there."

"I cannot have people seeing the two of you walking into her room together," Mr. Ackles protested.

"You just offered to let me stay in her room." Rhys reminded him.

"Walking in there together when everyone can see is different."

"I'm not going anywhere with you," she said, afraid if she stayed longer, let him explain himself, she would fall for his lies all over again. Just looking at him made her remember the joy she'd felt when they were together. She couldn't allow herself that weakness again.

She turned, and he caught her good arm.

"I had to go. I had to get Colby to jail."

She leveled a gaze at him. "And you had to lie to me, day after day. You had to take me to bed."

"Wait, wait, wait!" The proprietor put a hand on Rhys's arm. "You cannot have this conversation here. I have respectable people here. Perhaps you can use my personal parlor to continue this conversation."

"I have nothing more to say to him." Maddy pulled free, when all she wanted to do was turn into his chest and let him hold her, let him tell her more lies.

"Maddy. Please. I came back for you. I came back because I love you."

She pivoted toward him then. She wished he'd never said those words, not when she was so angry with him. She resented him for saying them, for manipulating her one more time. "Love me? How could that be? Nothing was real."

He reached for her other arm, and stopped himself before he aggravated her injury. "Everything was real. All of it."

"Except I thought you were a simple cowboy and you're a marshal who needed me to arrest an outlaw."

"I never intended to stay so long, to feel what I felt for you. I never intended to use you."

"You didn't trust me enough to tell me why you were there." And that was the part that hurt worst. "Without trust, how can there be love?"

"I wanted to tell you, but I couldn't."

"Why not?" Her voice rang shrilly in the entryway.

"Why couldn't you tell me? Did you think I would warn him?"

"At first I wasn't sure, out of loyalty, but later, no. No, I didn't think you would."

"So why couldn't you tell me?"

"I didn't know how, without hurting you. And when I finally knew what to say, it was too late."

"You're right," she said, struggling not to see the sorrow etched on his face. "It's too late." She pulled away and hurried up the stairs, part of her hoping he'd follow.

He didn't.

MADDY PRESSED a cool cloth to her eyes the following morning, but nothing she did could hide the fact that she'd cried all night. She was tempted to call for breakfast in her room, but she'd threatened Mr. Ackles that she'd eat every meal in the dining room until he arranged for a ride home for her. One thing she'd learned from the Colby brothers—always follow through on threats.

So she dressed, brushed her hair, straightened her shoulders and marched downstairs.

The first person she saw when she walked in the dining room was Rhys, sitting at the center table, leaning back in his chair, one long leg stretched in front of him as he nursed a cup of coffee. Her traitorous heart did a dance of excitement before she quelled it, looking away from him to find an available table.

There were none. She took a step back, prepared to order breakfast in her room, when Rhys saw her and stood.

"Good morning, Maddy," he said quietly.

For some reason she heard the words in the more intimate way, when he'd murmured them from the next pillow.

"Can we talk?"

She lifted her chin. "I just came in to get some breakfast, not to make another scene." What little reputation she had would never recover from last night's.

"I understand." He stepped aside. "Why don't you take my table?"

She hadn't realized she'd braced for an argument until none came. She certainly didn't expect to be disappointed. She nodded once and he dipped his head in farewell.

Nothing on the menu appealed to her, so she picked at her biscuits, frustration growing. Finally she pushed back her chair and stormed out of the dining room.

"Where can I find the marshal?" she demanded of Mr. Ackles.

"He went down to the livery stable, I believe."

She charged toward the door, hearing him say something else but not paying attention. Only when she was halfway down the sidewalk did his words register.

"You should take a coat."

Maddy hunched her shoulders against the cold, since she didn't have a coat with her in any case, and continued on. The livery stable was at the edge of town, but thankfully the town wasn't very big. Nonetheless, she was shivering when she pushed through the door.

Rhys stood with the livery owner, and turned his head when she charged in. He, of course, was dressed appropriately for the weather, in a bulky shearling coat and gloves.

"Maddy, what the hell?" he demanded, crossing to her, shrugging out of his coat and wrapping it around her shoulders.

"I decided I do want to talk," she said, willing her teeth not to chatter as the warmth from his coat sank into her skin.

"All right. I was coming back to the hotel. Why don't you go and we'll talk there?"

"I want to talk now. I want to know why you think you're better than Luke and Edward."

He raised his eyebrows. "I don't rob banks and kill people."

The image of him killing Tim Givens in her yard, a bullet between his eyes, returned, but that wasn't what she was here to argue.

"You took advantage of me, of my hospitality, of my trust. You wanted to get your man, and screwing me was just a bonus."

His cheeks reddened and he glanced at the livery owner, who backed away, giving them the illusion of privacy.

"I made love to you because I couldn't help myself,"

Rhys said, his voice low. "You are so pretty and so giving and so damned easy to fall for. I didn't mean to lie to you. I didn't want to lie to you. But my job was to get Colby back to Lubbock. I've never put anything ahead of my job, and I was wrong this time. You mean more to me than my badge, and I never wanted to see you hurt." His gaze flicked to her shoulder.

"But you did hurt me. I thought you were different. I thought you were someone I could depend on. I thought I knew you, but I don't. I don't know anything about the real man, the marshal."

"You do. Everything I told you about myself, about my life, that was real. I don't know how many ways I can say I'm sorry I didn't tell you myself. All I can do is show you. Let me take you home, let me take care of you."

"I don't need someone to take care of me. I want someone who will be my partner. That's what I thought I'd have with you."

"Then I'll be that. Let me have another chance to make it right."

She looked up at him, into his eyes, and saw sincerity there. Was she a fool to want to believe him? Would she end up being hurt again? Cautiously she said, "I'll let you take me home. Beyond that, I won't make any promises."

MADDY WAS SHIVERING with more than the cold when they crested the hill overlooking her house. Rhys had been unfailingly polite to her, which only made her more uncomfortable. Would they ever find the ease they'd once had? Or was she hoping for too much?

The questions stopped abruptly when she saw the scene below her. "What happened to my house?"

The front was the same, except now it was white-washed, as were the barn and chicken coop. But the house itself had—grown.

"Some of my friends came to help me," he said, urging the horses down the hill faster than was probably wise. "We tore out the back wall and added a bedroom and an indoor privy."

She turned on the seat to face him. "No."

A grin creased his face. "Yes. We placed Spanish tile on the floor and a drain, and I was able to find one of those toilets in Lubbock." He pulled the horse up in front of the cabin and hurried around to help her down.

She could feel the eagerness running through his body as he drew her toward the door. When he swung it open, she was surprised by the emptiness of the room without her bed in the center, and the curtained-off chamber pot and basin were missing. New wood created the far wall, and a door was set into it. Rhys took her good hand and tugged her toward the new room.

He opened the door and she could barely catch her breath. A new dresser sat beside her bed, and a wood stove was on the other side, its pipe vented through a hole in the ceiling. Something was wrapped around the pipe, and when she looked closer, she saw it was a narrow copper pipe.

"It's to heat the water for the tub," he said. "You don't have to carry it from the kitchen anymore." Then he drew back a curtain to reveal a privy three times the size of the one in the hotel.

A copper tub sat beside the wood stove, and the pipe from the stove led directly to it, as did another pipe from the ceiling. He leaned over to indicate the taps. "This for hot water," he showed her, twisting the knob. "This for cold."

"The hotel had one of these," she murmured, stroking the new appliance in wonder before turning to the next. A toilet sat on the adjoining wall, a tank overhead.

Rhys crossed to it and pulled the cord attached to the tank, and together they watched the water disappear from the bowl.

"Where does it go?" she asked.

"I dug a trench downhill, and it will collect in an underground tank that will need to be limed on occasion, especially during the summer. And this—" He gestured to the corner of the room, lined with Spanish tiles, except for a grated hole in the middle. A modified bucket sat high on a shelf.

"An indoor shower," she breathed.

"You'll have to get the warm water from the tub, but it will be less work than heating it in the sink. And it will drain into a cistern in the yard, so we can reuse the water for your garden."

"How did you—where did you get all this?" she asked, turning in a circle, trying to take it all in.

"I got a fee for bringing in Colby."

And he spent it on her house, not knowing if she would forgive him.

"I haven't had a home since Polly died," he went on when she didn't say anything. "This place is the first place I wanted to come back to. You were the first woman since her that I wanted to make a home with. So I made you a home."

"That was a big gamble."

"It was a chance I was willing to take." He took another then, and stepped closer, brushing his knuckle down her cheek. "Tell me it paid off. Tell me I can stay. There will be no more secrets, no more lies."

Her heart swelled as she looked into his sincere brown eyes. "You can stay, on two conditions."

He caught his breath, waiting.

"You help me get into that tub. And you tell me you love me again."

He scooped her hair back from her face. "I love you, Maddy Colby. That's no lie."

And he kissed her, long and sweet. The tub had to wait.

ABOUT THE AUTHOR

Emma Jay has been writing longer than she'd care to admit, using her endless string of celebrity crushes as inspiration for her heroes. Emma, married 35 years (wed at the age of 8, of course) believes writing romance is like falling in love, over and over again. Creating characters and love stories is an addiction she has no intention of breaking.